# THE COOKIE THIEF
# Girl Scout
# MYSTERY

## by Carole Marsh

First Edition ©2016 Carole Marsh/Gallopade International/Peachtree City, GA
Current Edition ©November 2017
Ebook edition ©2016
All rights reserved.
Manufactured in Peachtree City, GA

Carole Marsh Mysteries™ and its skull colophon are the property of Carole Marsh and
Gallopade International.

Published by Gallopade International/Carole Marsh Books. Printed in the United States
of America.

Managing Editor: Janice Baker
Assistant Editor: Whitney Akin
Cover Design: John Hanson
Content Design: John Hanson

*Gallopade is proud to be a member and supporter of these educational
organizations and associations:*

**American Booksellers Association**
**American Library Association**
**International Reading Association**
**National Association for Gifted Children**
**The National School Supply and Equipment Association**
**The National Council for the Social Studies**
**Museum Store Association**
**Association of Partners for Public Lands**
**Association of Booksellers for Children**
**Association for the Study of African American Life and History**
**National Alliance of Black School Educators**

4

Dear Readers,

Who doesn't love Girl Scout Cookies? The familiar annual sight of smiling, cheerful Girl Scouts selling cookies to raise money for good causes always warms my heart. And I never hesitate to fill my pantry (and  freezer) with boxes and boxes to feed Papa's sweet tooth. (And I just may sneak a cookie or two for myself!)

In this book, the third in our Girl Scout Mystery series, you'll ride along with a great group of Girl Scouts as they sell, sell, sell...and have fun, fun, fun!

But besides having fun and raising money, Girl Scouts learn many valuable life lessons and business skills while selling those tasty cookies. Things like setting goals, planning, managing money, working with people, and making good decisions are precious "know-how" you will use for the rest of your lives!

My advice? Grab a glass of milk and a handful of Girl Scout Cookies, and dig into *The Cookie Thief Girl Scout Mystery!* It's truly a "sweet treat"!

*Carole Marsh*

# TABLE OF CONTENTS

# 1

# LOOKIE, LOOKIE, WE'VE GOT COOKIES!

"This makes me so mad! I can't get this cookie to fit over my head," Ella grumbled. She hopped around her bedroom, trying to force a cardboard cutout of a caramel cookie over her head and shoulders.

"I think you're supposed to *step* into it," Ella's friend Annie suggested. Her dark, silky brown hair was woven into a loose braid tied with a green ribbon. The ribbon glittered with multicolored sprinkled cookies printed all over it. The colors popped against her olive skin. Annie wore an empty shortbread cookie box over her waist held up with red suspenders.

"Well, you could have told me that before I got my shoulders stuck!" Ella complained. She yanked the cookie cutout off her head and stepped into the hole in the middle, easily pulling it up to her waist. "There! A cookie skirt!"

Ella and Annie twirled around to admire their outfits in Ella's full-length mirror. Along with the "cookie skirt," Ella wore polka-dotted socks pulled up to her knees, her Girl Scout vest, and the same cookie-print ribbon in her long, straight blond hair as Annie had. Annie wore cutouts of different types of Girl Scout Cookies pinned to her shirt. Both girls grabbed noisemakers made out of empty milk bottles filled with beans.

"I think we're ready!" Ella exclaimed. She was proud of their creative outfit ideas!

"Whoa! You two are really taking this parade thing seriously." Ella's older sister Avery burst into Ella's room without knocking, again. Her blonde hair flew into the air as she bounced onto Ella's bed.

Ella felt her cheeks turn red. "We're dressed for the cookie rally! I thought you and Kate were dressing up too!"

"Usually only the Brownies dress in silly outfits," Avery replied. She and her friend Kate eyed each other and laughed.

Ella considered wriggling out of her "cookie skirt." She didn't want to look like a silly, naive Brownie. She glanced back into the mirror and changed her mind. "I think we look cute," she declared.

"It's almost time!" Annie's excited announcement interrupted Ella's thoughts. "The rally starts in ten minutes." Annie grabbed Ella's hand with a squeal and pulled her out of the bedroom.

The girls headed downstairs to a living room full of other Girl Scouts. Ella and Avery had volunteered their house as the meeting place for their cookie parade. They lived two blocks from the community center where a giant cookie rally party was set up. Their troop planned to host a mini parade from Ella and Avery's house to the community center to mark the kick-off of cookie-selling season. Mimi and Papa, the girls' grandparents, had offered to chaperone the parade. They were visiting from their home in South Carolina. Mimi wrote children's mystery books for a living and always had a flair for the dramatic. She had spent all day decorating the community center with other volunteers. Ella couldn't wait to see what it looked like.

"OK, Girl Scouts, let's line up!" called Mrs. Graham, Ella and Avery's troop leader. She waved her hands over her head to direct the girls to the front door. "We will proceed youngest to oldest, so Brownies first."

Ella and Annie scrambled to the front of the line with the other Brownies, their noisemakers poised high in the air. The older scouts filed in behind them, including Avery and Kate. While she wasn't as excited as her little sister was, Avery couldn't hide the smile that spread across her face. Cookie-selling season was her favorite part about being a Girl Scout!

"Let's go!" Mrs. Graham opened the door and stepped out in an animated march. She led the girls along the sidewalk toward the community center. Several chaperones, including Mimi and Papa, walked on either side of the Girl Scouts to make sure they were safe.

Ella and Annie shook their noisemakers as hard as they could above their heads. One of the Junior Scouts yelled, "Lookie, lookie, we've got cookies!" The others echoed the cheer over and over as they marched down the sidewalk. Several drivers passing by honked their horns in support. Others leaned out their windows and waved to the girls.

Papa grinned and tipped his black cowboy hat in reply. "Just moving these little cowpokes along to their cookie party," he called to the drivers. Mimi laughed. "Remember, it's not about you, Papa," she said. "It's all about the cookies!"

Ella was breathless with excitement when the girls arrived at the community center.

"That was so much fun!" Annie squealed. "We should have parades more often!"

"And it's not over yet," Ella added. "We still get to go to the cookie rally. I can't wait to see what Mimi did with the decorations. Believe me, it'll be good!"

Annie and Ella grinned as Mrs. Graham pulled open the double doors of the community center. "Welcome to our 10th annual Girl Scout Cookie Rally!" she announced.

# 2

## AUNTIE MANURE

Ella sucked in a deep breath as the doors opened. The community center had several small rooms situated around one massive gymnasium used for community sports, parties, and political events. But Ella had never seen the gym like this before. Colorful banners for each ranking of Girl Scouts draped the walls of the gym. Ella quickly found the brown Brownie banner and gathered under it with the other Brownies. Avery and Kate headed toward the green Junior banner. Twinkling multicolored lights hung from the ceiling, adding a warm feeling to the normally plain gym. A Girl Scout logo made of banner paper was taped to the wall in the middle of the other banners.

A long table in the center of the gym held a huge spread of food. Ella's eyes feasted on saucy meatballs, pigs in a blanket, crispy chicken nuggets, vegetable trays, a colorful fruit platter, and plates of every kind of Girl Scout Cookie.

"That's a lot of cookies!" Ella whispered to Annie.

Smaller tables dotted the outer walls of the gym. Each was decorated with a different cookie-related theme.

"Welcome Girl Scouts, families, and friends!" Mrs. Graham stood under the Girl Scout banners with a microphone. "We are so excited for a new season of cookie selling! This Cookie Rally is our way of kicking off this exciting season and letting the community know that the Girl Scout Cookies are FINALLY HERE!" Mrs. Graham said the last words in a high-pitched sing-song voice, and the crowd in the gym cheered.

"Please enjoy some great food," Mrs. Graham added. "We invite our Girl Scouts to visit all of our cookie-selling stations set up around the room. Each table has a special ribbon you can pin to your vest to show you completed your cookie-selling prep courses. Remember, you're never too old to review the best ways to sell our delicious Girl Scout Cookies!" Mrs. Graham looked at Avery and Kate's group with a smile.

"OK, now, go have fun!" Mrs. Graham excitedly applauded and the rest of the gym joined her.

"Where should we go first?" Annie asked. She grabbed Ella's hand and they scanned the room together.

"THERE!" Ella exclaimed. She pointed to a table in the corner decorated with a bright red tablecloth dotted with glitter and sparkly red balloons. "That has got to be the table Mimi decorated!"

As the girls neared the table, they spotted a sign above it that said, "Cookie Selling Safety Tips." Mimi stood behind the table in a red sequin top with a shiny gemstone cookie pinned just below her right shoulder.

"Mimi! Your table looks great," Ella said.

"Thank you, sweetie." Mimi leaned down and gave Ella a big kiss on the cheek, leaving behind a bright red lipstick mark. Ella quickly wiped her cheek with her sleeve.

"My table is all about cookie-selling safety," Mimi explained. "I picked this theme because it's so important to me that my little angels are safe!"

"Are these safety rules like you should look both ways before crossing the street?" asked Annie.

"Sure, that could be one," Mimi said, "but there are others too. There are some really important ones like always wear your Girl Scout uniform when selling cookies so that people know who you are. Another rule is always have a buddy when selling cookies. You never do it alone."

Annie and Ella looped elbows and grinned up at Mimi.

"Good, I see you've already found a buddy," Mimi said. "Here's a handout that lists some of our most important rules." Mimi handed the girls a brochure with safety tips.

"It says here to partner with adults, too," Ella read.

"That's right! That's why I volunteered to chaperone," Mimi announced with a smile. "I get to go with you when you sell cookies door-to-door."

Ella wasn't sure if she was excited or disappointed. She loved being with Mimi, but she was looking forward to being a grown-up, independent Girl Scout.

"Don't worry, I'll let you do all the work," Mimi said. She winked at Ella. "Here, take the brochure with you and review the safety rules before you start selling. And here are your ribbons!" Mimi handed both girls a gold button with a sparkly red ribbon attached. The button read "SAFETY RULES." Annie and Ella proudly pinned the button to their vests and headed to the next table.

An hour later, Annie and Ella had ribbons all over their vests and a handful of handouts. They had visited tables featuring how to handle money, how to market their cookie selling, how to set cookie-selling goals, and how to use the digital cookie app.

Ella stared down at a handout that looked like a game board. Each step of the cookie-selling process was mapped out on the sheet, from goal setting to how to use your cookie money. The steps in between included holding a meeting with family and friends, finding good cookie-selling spots, and tracking your progress.

*I hope I can do this*, Ella thought.

"Man, this is a lot more work than I thought," Annie commented.

Ella nodded, "It's almost like running a business!"

"That's the whole point," Avery chimed in. She and Kate had visited tables and added ribbons to their vests as well. "Cookie selling is about a lot more than just having fun. And it sure is a LOT of fun!"

"Yeah, one day I want to be an entrepreneur," Kate said. She firmly nodded her brunette head.

"An auntie manure? What is that?" Annie asked, scrunching her nose in disgust.

"An entre-pre-neur," Kate said slowly. "It's someone who starts their own business. Cookie selling has taught me some important lessons to help with that, like how to handle money and market a product."

Ella still felt uneasy about the job before her.

"Don't worry, my little sis, I'll be here to help you," Avery said. "We'll follow the five steps to success and you just might get a Cookie Activity Pin by the time we're done." She winked at Ella.

Most of the time Ella thought she just embarrassed her older sister, but once in a while Avery surprised her. Ella felt a sense of relief knowing Avery would be there to help her with her first cookie-selling season.

"You guys haven't been to the best table yet," Kate said. She pointed toward a table covered with towers of colorful boxes. A sign above it said, "Cookie Tasting Station."

As they headed toward the mountain of fresh Girl Scout Cookies, Mrs. Graham's voice bellowed over the microphone again.

"I have a special announcement for all my favorite Girl Scouts!" she declared. "Sweet Treat Bakery is opening up a brand new cookie plant near our town. They are the newest baker selected to bake and package Girl Scout Cookies. This special honor is only given to three bakeries in the entire United States!" Some of Girl Scouts began to applaud.

"Oh, that's not even the best news!" Mrs. Graham said. She was breathless with excitement. "A representative from the bakery just informed me that our troop has been chosen for an exclusive, behind-the-scenes tour to see how our favorite cookies are made!"

The entire gym broke out in applause. Ella and Annie grabbed hands and jumped up and down.

Avery giggled at her little sister and said, "You're such a Brownie, Ella." But deep down, Avery was excited, too.

# 3

# SWEET TREAT

The Sweet Treat Bakery was only an hour's drive away. The girls met to drive there in a caravan of minivans and SUVs. Mimi offered to drive her two-door red Cadillac, but she could only take two girls. Avery and Ella convinced her to take the family minivan instead. "Hey, Mimi, we can call it the 'Mimi-van' after you," Ella had suggested. Mimi wasn't crazy about minivans, but she liked that idea!

Mimi, Mrs. Graham, Avery, Kate, Annie, and Ella all piled in to the newly named "Mimi-van." The vehicle buzzed with excitement.

"I can't believe they picked *our* troop!" Avery said. "I can't wait to see how the cookies are made!"

23

"Do you think they'll let us mix a batch?" Annie almost squealed as she asked the question.

"I don't think so," Mrs. Graham replied. "Every Girl Scout Cookie bakery has strict health and safety codes. The recipes are closely followed so every cookie is a delicious treat. People love their Girl Scout Cookies, so it's important to make them exactly the same every time."

"Oh," Annie said, slightly disappointed.

"But you'll get to watch a batch being mixed, I'm sure," Mrs. Graham continued. "And the representative told me the tour comes with a complimentary cookie sample at the end."

"Oooh, I'm going to choose chocolate mint!" Ella declared.

As Mimi drove down the four-lane highway, the buildings outside vanished in the distance. The cityscape turned into open fields with barbed wire fencing and black and brown cows.

"This place is really in the boonies!" Mimi commented.

To pass the time, Ella pulled out the worksheet she'd gotten the other night at the cookie-selling rally. "I guess I need to start thinking about my cookie-selling strategy," she said.

"Speaking of strategy, do you guys have any idea of what project we could do for our Bronze Award?" Ella asked, changing the subject. "I really want to earn it this year!"

"I may have an idea," Annie said. "You know my little sister has to be in a wheelchair. I was wondering if we could do something to help her and other handicapped people."

"That's a great idea, Annie," Kate said. "What were you thinking?"

"Well, she loves to look at the lake from the park," Annie replied. "You know that gazebo up on the hill?"

"I do," Avery said. "That's my favorite place to go when we visit the park. The view is so peaceful and beautiful."

"I know!" Annie said. "But it makes me sad because my sister can't enjoy it. There's no wheelchair ramp into the gazebo. I was thinking maybe we could use the money from our cookie sales to build a ramp."

"That's a wonderful idea!" Mrs. Graham said. "I couldn't help but hear what you suggested, Annie, and I can't think of a better way for our troop to give back to the community!"

"Really?" Annie said.

"Absolutely," Mrs. Graham declared. "I would encourage you to share the idea with the troop. Explain the idea, how you will complete the project, and what problem it will solve in the community. Then we can take a vote to see if the other girls would like to pursue a wheelchair ramp as the Bronze Award project."

"That would be awesome, Annie!" Ella said.

"Look!" Avery pointed out the window to a sign that read, "Sweet Treat Bakery" in bright pink and green letters.

"We're here, girls!" Mimi announced.

They drove toward a reddish brick building surrounded by a massive parking lot and green fields on all sides. A few long, skinny windows flanked the front entrance. On the side of the building, white delivery trucks with pink and green logos were backed up to tall square openings where workers loaded pallets of cookie boxes into them.

The caravan of cars parked in the expansive front parking lot. Mrs. Graham organized the Girl Scouts into lines and led them toward the front entrance.

A tall, thin man with jet black hair and a big smile held the door open for the visitors.

"Welcome to Sweet Treat Bakery!" he announced. "We are honored to have your troop visit our bakery. I am Mr. Turner."

"Thank *you*, Mr. Turner." Mrs. Graham stretched out her arm to shake his hand. "We are all so excited to tour your factory."

"Wonderful!" Mr. Turner led the girls into a large lobby and through a double door marked, "Authorized Personnel Only." "We'll start our tour in the bakery," he added.

"I feel like I'm going behind the scenes on a movie!" Ella whispered to Annie.

The girls entered a huge, white room with a maze of machines. Immense metal pots rotated, mixing dry ingredients. Other pots with claw-like mixers blended wet ingredients. Tray after tray of cookies rode on a long conveyor belt into ovens. Workers in white coats and hair nets worked diligently at stations around the bakery.

Ella paused to take it all in. She'd helped Mimi bake cookies before, but this was nothing like that. This was the biggest bakery and the most cookies she'd ever seen! The room hummed and clicked with the sound of gleaming silver machines.

Just as she was about to follow Mr. Turner deeper into the bakery, something caught Ella's eye. A woman in a white coat and hair net held a plastic bag over a pot of wet ingredients. Little black morsels poured into the mixture, but the side of the pot said SHORTBREAD in big block letters. Ella nudged Annie with her elbow.

"Either someone changed the original Girl Scout Cookie recipe, or that lady just made a BIG mistake," Ella whispered.

"You're right," Annie said. "It looks like she's going to ruin those shortbread cookies!"

# 4

# BOTCHED BATCH

Ella and Annie could hardly focus on the rest of the bakery tour. They half-listened as Mr. Turner told them how the dry ingredients like flour, sugar, and salt mix together in a big metal pot. Then the dry ingredients were added to the wet ingredients like butter, milk, and flavorings. Mr. Turner explained how each cookie had its own unique baking process.

"Each recipe is carefully followed to give our customers their favorite cookies," Mr. Turner said. "All of our ingredients are fresh and of the highest quality."

"Did you hear that?" Annie whispered to Ella. "He said, 'Each recipe is carefully followed.'"

"Yes," Ella said. "I think we should say something to him."

"I don't want to get that lady in trouble, though," Annie said.

"Me neither," Ella answered. "But people just can't get wrong Girl Scout Cookies!"

"Maybe they created a new flavor and it's a secret," Annie suggested. "We don't know for sure that she made a mistake."

Mr. Turner led the group toward the packaging process where cardboard boxes adorned with pictures of Girl Scouts were stacked into larger cardboard boxes to be shipped across the southeastern United States.

"Maybe you're right," Ella decided.

She turned her attention back to Mr. Turner when suddenly, a loud alarm sounded across the bakery. RING! RING! RING! The clicking and buzzing sounds of the machines came to an **abrupt** stop. The employees stopped what they were doing. Except for the high-pitched whirring of the alarm, the bakery was silent. Muffled voices sounded over Mr. Turner's walkie-talkie.

"Say that again?" Mr. Turner said into the speaker.

"We have a botched batch." Annie and Ella could hear the voice on the walkie-talkie loud and clear.

Mr. Turner asked the girls to wait and walked a few steps away so Annie and Ella could only hear his side of the conversation. He spoke urgently into the walkie-talkie.

"How many?"

"How did they get out of the bakery?"

"Are we sure the truck has already left?"

"We have to get them back here. We can't risk customers getting a botched batch."

"I understand."

Mr. Turner cleared his throat and returned to his visitors. "I'm very sorry, girls, but I'm going to have to cut our tour short. Please proceed back to the entrance to get your complimentary sample."

Mrs. Graham ushered the troop back through the double doors to the lobby.

"That sounded pretty serious," Avery said. "I wonder what happened."

"We saw it!" Annie gushed.

"What?!" Kate exclaimed. "What did you see?"

"A lady added chocolate morsels to a batch of shortbread cookies," Ella explained. "I knew it had to be a **mishap** when I saw SHORTBREAD written on the side of the pot she was using."

"Hmmm, chocolate shortbread doesn't sound too bad," Kate said.

"That's not the point," Avery said. She looked concerned. "Girl Scout Cookies are a tradition. The first Girl Scout sugar cookies were made in 1922! You can't just change a recipe. If someone gets shortbread cookies with chocolate chips, it's not a real Girl Scout Cookie."

"Do you think she did it on purpose?" Annie asked.

Ella looked at Annie and shrugged her shoulders. "I don't know!" she replied.

Her thoughts were interrupted when a bakery worker burst through the double doors with silver trays of Girl Scout Cookies.

"We have five flavors to choose from..." The worker said. Her blonde hair was still visible under her pink hair net. "They are chocolate mint, shortbread, caramel coconut, chocolate peanut butter, and lemon. When you get your cookie boxes to sell, look closely at the code on the bottom near the bar code. That tells you which factory baked that batch. Our bakery code is SWTTRT123. If you see that on the bottom of your boxes you know they were made here!" The perky worker handed out cookies to each of the Girl Scouts.

As the girls piled back into the minivan and settled in for the drive home, Ella's mind couldn't help but go back to the lady in the factory.

*Would they find all the cookies?  Would the lady get in trouble?*

But one thought nagged at the back of her mind.

*Did she ruin the batch on purpose?*

# 5

# SELLING STRATEGIES

Ella felt like she was going through the motions of her Monday activities at school. She still wondered about the factory **fiasco,** but she was too busy creating cookie-selling strategies to focus on the botched batch. She couldn't wait to get to the county library for her first Girl Scout meeting of cookie-selling season. Tonight Mrs. Graham would review each girl's goals, discuss selling strategies, and distribute boxes to sell.

Ella had set a personal goal of selling 200 boxes and she couldn't wait to tell Mrs. Graham. She knew it would be a challenge, but she wanted to prove she could rock her first cookie season!

When 5:30 finally rolled around, Ella rushed through the doors of the local library and into the front conference room where the troop met each week. She quickly found Annie and took a seat in the folding chairs.

"Welcome, girls," Mrs. Graham said to quiet the excited group. "I know we're all ready to start selling these delicious cookies! However, we must do first things first. Tonight's meeting will be a little different. I will meet with each of you to discuss your goals, assign partners, and assign boxes. You will all have to wait for your turn tonight, so please be patient. And try to keep your volume to a dull roar, ladies!"

Mrs. Graham started calling girls whose first name started with A, calling Addy Earnest first.

"You'll get to go before me," Ella told Annie. "Tell her we want to be partners."

"Definitely!" Annie smiled.

Ella watched Annie and Avery meet with Mrs. Graham. Her name started with the fifth letter of the alphabet, but it felt like 50 before Mrs. Graham got to her letter. Finally, she heard loud and clear, "Ella."

Ella rushed toward the front of the room where Mrs. Graham sat at a plastic table smothered with papers.

"Now, Ella," Mrs. Graham said, putting a check next to Ella's name on a list. "Have you thought about your personal cookie-selling goals?"

"Yes," Ella replied. "I'd like to try to sell 200 boxes."

"That's a wonderful goal, Ella," Mrs. Graham smiled. "How do you plan to sell those boxes?"

Ella took a deep breath. "I've been looking at my worksheets from the rally and I think I want to sell them in a couple of ways," she explained. "First, I'll send order forms to my close family and friends by email. Then, I plan to sell cookies at cookie booths in front of local stores. I'll also put some in a wagon and do a Cookie Walkabout with other Girl Scouts in some neighborhoods."

"That sounds like a good plan," Mrs. Graham said. "I am confident you'll be able to sell all of your boxes! First you'll need your order form." Mrs. Graham handed Ella a long, colorful form to list customer names and cookie choices. "Then you'll need to make sure you have a partner when you're selling at the grocery store," she added. "Annie said you'd like to be together. Is that OK with you?"

"Yes, ma'am!" Ella said quickly.

"Great! Now we need to go over the safety rules for door-to-door selling." Mrs. Graham handed another paper to Ella and looked her in the eye. "You need to plan which area you would like to sell in. You need to always be with an adult and a partner. Never go inside someone's home and always wear your Girl Scout uniform."

"OK, I can do that," Ella said, nodding.

"Now, let me assign you some boxes of cookies so you can get started," Mrs. Graham continued. "I'll give you a variety to start with and when you run out, you can restock with me as needed. I'll start you out with 20 boxes, so let's see here..." Mrs. Graham leaned over and rummaged through a big cardboard box on the floor. "Huh, that's odd," she said. "I'm almost out of boxes and I have several more girls to get through. I ordered enough for each girl to start with 20 boxes. I'm not sure what happened."

Mrs. Graham looked concerned. "I'm sorry, Ella, I'm only going to be able to give you five boxes for now. I know that's not much, but it will at least get you started. You can restock with me soon."

Ella nodded, stuffed the boxes in the grocery bag she brought, and walked back to her seat.

"How'd it go?" Annie asked.

"Fine." Ella didn't want her friend to see how disappointed she was.

"What's wrong?" Annie asked. She could see the frown on Ella's face.

"I only got five boxes to sell," Ella complained. She showed Annie her bag. "At this rate, I'll never reach my goal."

"Mrs. Graham gave me 20," Annie said. "I wonder why she gave you less."

"She said she didn't have enough boxes," Ella explained. "She acted confused and didn't know where they'd gone."

"Our cookies have gone missing?" Annie said.

"I guess," Ella replied. She felt defeated before she could even sell her first box of cookies.

Avery and Kate plopped down in the empty seats next to Annie. "Hey, Ella, ready to get selling?" Avery asked cheerily. Avery's bag overflowed with cookie boxes.

"She only got five boxes," Annie said. "By the time Mrs. Graham calls Kate's name, she probably won't have any left."

"She didn't order enough boxes?" Avery said. "That's strange, Mrs. Graham always orders more than enough boxes."

"She said she did," Ella said. "But now she can't find the rest."

"Look!" Kate exclaimed. She pointed to the massive arched window overlooking the library's front parking lot. "That looks like one of the delivery trucks we saw at Sweet Treat Bakery."

Outside, a white truck with a bright green and pink logo was parked next to the sidewalk in front of the library.

"Maybe Mrs. Graham didn't get all the boxes out of the truck," Annie suggested.

Ella perked up. "We could go look," she suggested. "Maybe I can get my quota of boxes after all," she whispered to herself.

The four girls agreed and quietly slipped out of the conference room while Mrs. Graham met with Gabby and the rest of the G names.

The back of the delivery truck door was still propped open. The girls warily peeked in at the towers of stacked cardboard boxes.

"How do we know which ones are for our troop?" Avery asked.

"These boxes say SU509. Hey, that's a troop number!" Kate noticed.

"I think I see some that say SU617. That's our troop number, isn't it, Avery?" Ella asked. She squinted at the boxes in the back of the truck.

"Yes!" Avery said. "Mrs. Graham must have missed some boxes. How many are there?"

"I can't tell, give me a boost," Ella said. Kate and Avery hoisted Ella into the back of the truck.

"Yep, definitely SU617!" Ella said. "Can you guys help me get them out? Mrs. Graham will be so relieved!"

Annie, Avery, and Kate jumped into the back of the truck with Ella.

"See, right here..." Ella began. BANG! The inside of the truck went black. Annie shrieked. The sliding back door to the truck had slammed shut!

The girls heard footsteps to the side of the truck, then the engine starting.

"Oh no, the driver doesn't know we're back here!" Ella whispered, her voice shaking.

# 6

## RAT RACE

The delivery truck let out a long groan as the driver hoisted the gears into drive. The truck lurched forward.

"Brace yourselves!" Avery yelled. The truck made a wide turn and the girls slid and tumbled against a tower of cookie boxes.

"What are we going to do? We can't go all the way back to the bakery!" Annie cried. Her voice was breathless with fear and a rush of adrenaline.

"AHHHHHHH!" Kate's scream echoed off the metal walls of the truck. "Something just touched me! I think it was A RAT!"

"What!?" Avery yelled over Kate's screaming. "There can't be a..."

"A RAAAAAAT!" Ella screamed, her high-pitched voice mixing in with Kate's screaming.

"It just touched me too, Avery!" Ella yelled. She scampered to the corner of the truck and tried to curl herself into a ball.

"It was slimy and warm and I felt a long tail wrap around my leg," Ella explained, shivering. The delivery truck made another sharp turn and all the girls screamed, imagining a rat scrambling around their feet.

"I *CAN'T* be in a van with a rat. I just can't," Annie started repeating loudly. "I hate rats! I hate rats!"

"We've got to get out of here," Avery said, her voice shaky, but at a normal volume. "Everyone stay calm..."

WHAM! A huge bump tossed the girls up toward the ceiling, interrupting Avery. They landed with a THUD.

"HEEEEEELLLLLPPPP," Ella started screaming. "Help us, we're stuck back here!"

Kate started banging on the metal sides of the truck.

"I HATE RATS!!!" Annie kept yelling.

Avery dug through her pockets to see if she had her phone. Just then, the truck came to an abrupt stop. The girls jerked toward the wall.

"Ouch!" Ella cried.

Seconds later the back door of the truck swung open sharply.

"What in tarnation is going on back here?" A heavyset woman in a blue button-down blouse stood in the blinding sunlight. Her thin, gray hair was pulled into a messy bun. When she talked, the girls saw a noticeable gap separating her front two teeth.

"Um, we're trapped," Ella answered cautiously.

"Trapped?" The woman frowned. "How did you get back here? This is my truck, and you shouldn't have been snooping around."

"We weren't snooping..." Avery said. "We're sorry..."

"OUT!" the woman shouted. "Out of my truck now. I've got a long drive ahead of me. You need to call someone to come pick you up."

The girls crouched and stepped gingerly toward the back door.

"EEEEK!" Kate screamed again.

"THE RAT!" Annie cried, pushing the other girls aside to get out of the truck.

"Rat? What are you talking about?" the woman snapped. She opened the back door wider to let more light in. A stringy wet mop lay limp on the truck floor. "There are no rats in my truck, young ladies. I keep a clean vehicle!"

Ella stared at the mop, her mind racing with relief and embarrassment. *Was THAT the rat?* She eyed Annie, and after a shared look of humiliation, they let out a giggle.

"I'll call Mimi," Avery said. She found her phone in her back pocket and dialed her grandmother.

"We are very sorry to mess up your delivery route, ma'am," Annie said. She tried to break the awkward silence while they waited for Mimi to rescue them.

"Humph," the woman grunted, her mouth turned down in a frown.

"I'm Annie, by the way," Annie said, holding out her hand. The woman gave no response. "What's your name?"

"You can call me Ms. Tara," the woman muttered.

"Nice to meet you, Ms. Tara," Annie said lightly. Ms. Tara furrowed her brow in annoyance.

As they waited for Mimi, Ella hung her legs off the back bumper of the truck and tapped her fingers over and over. She was trying to work up the confidence to talk to Ms. Tara.

"I think you still have some of our cookie boxes," Ella finally blurted out.

"Excuse me?" Ms. Tara seemed offended.

"I mean, our troop's boxes," Ella explained. "I mean, Mrs. Graham's boxes." Ella wished she'd kept silent, but it was too late now. "I thought I saw some boxes labeled with our troop number in the back of the truck. I think maybe Mrs. Graham didn't get all her boxes back at the library."

"I assure you she did," Ms. Tara snapped. "She must have ordered the wrong number of boxes. I don't make mistakes with my deliveries."

"But...," Ella continued. Avery eyed her little sister and Ella stopped talking.

*I know I saw our number,* Ella thought. She couldn't help but think Ms. Tara was either wrong or lying.

Finally, Mimi pulled up in Avery and Ella's mom's minivan.

"I'm so sorry, ma'am," Mimi said as she approached Ms. Tara. "Thank you for keeping an eye on my girls. This could have been a disaster!" Mimi scooped all four girls into a group hug. She looked at Avery. "And I want to know why you were in that truck," she whispered to her granddaughter.

As the other girls headed toward the minivan, Ella saw a piece of paper stuck between the delivery truck bumper and the door. She quickly snatched it before running to Mimi's van. Annie waved to Ms. Tara as they pulled away.  Ms. Tara stared back with a deep frown.  "Kids," she mumbled.

On the drive back to the library, Ella slowly unfolded the piece of paper she'd snatched. She gasped when she read the contents:

| Troop Number | Leader Name | Boxes per Girl Scout | # of Girl Scouts | Total |
|---|---|---|---|---|
| SU509 | Mrs. Williams | 15 | 25 | 375 |
| SU617 | Mrs. Graham | 20 | 19 | 380 |

Ella's mind was whirling.  It was an inventory list!  Mrs. Graham had ordered the right amount of cookies.  Ella had seen her troop number on boxes in the back of the truck.  And that meant only one thing: Ms. Tara had something to hide!

# 7

# COOKIE THIEF

Bright and early Saturday morning, the girls planned to go to Mega Mart, the largest grocery store in town, to sell cookies. The store agreed to let them set up a table right outside the main door so grocery shoppers could purchase cookies on their way in or out.

Annie and Kate slept over with Ella and Avery the night before so they could get ready for the sale.

"If we pool our resources together, we have at least fifty boxes," Avery calculated.

"And Mrs. Graham said she would try to bring some more inventory tomorrow afternoon in case we run out," Kate said.

"That's perfect," Ella chirped, "because I plan to sell lots of cookies tomorrow!"

"Me too!" Annie said. "I really want to reach our goal. Maybe we could use some of the money we earn to buy supplies to build the handicap ramp. I can't wait until my sister can enjoy that beautiful gazebo view."

"Well, you guys are Brownies, so Kate and I have more experience," Avery said in her best know-it-all voice. Ella rolled her eyes. "So I think we should give you a few cookie-selling pointers. Like, for starters, make sure you always smile!"

"And talk," Kate chimed in. "You have to speak up, be loud and courteous, and ask if people want to buy cookies. And make sure you ask *everyone* that walks by. You never know who might be a potential customer."

"Ella, this is important, are you listening?" Avery looked at her little sister who was staring at the wall.

"What? Oh, yeah, I'm listening. Smile. Talk," Ella muttered.

"This is important, Ella," Avery said again, annoyed.

"I know. I'm sorry, Avery, I just feel distracted," Ella said. She paused, not sure that she wanted to share her suspicions about Ms. Tara. She decided someone had to know. "I think Ms. Tara lied to us the other day."

"Who?" Kate looked confused.

"The delivery truck lady!" Annie exclaimed. "Have you forgotten our rat-tastic adventure already?" Annie giggled at her joke.

"Lied?" Avery said. "That's a strong accusation. Are you sure, Ella?" Avery wasn't laughing with Kate and Annie.

"She said Mrs. Graham ordered the wrong amount of cookies, but on my way out of the truck I found this." Ella handed Avery the inventory list.

"Oh man," Avery said.

"I don't understand," Annie remarked. She snatched the piece of paper from Avery and read it carefully.

"Why would she lie about having cookies?" Annie asked. "Isn't it her job to make sure *all* the cookies are delivered?"

"It doesn't make any sense, I know," Ella answered. "I've been thinking about it since Monday. But the facts are right here. I think we have a..."

"DON"T say it," Avery yelled. "Just because we have a strange situation does not mean we have one of *those*."

"Those? What are you girls talking about?" Kate asked.

"Don't say it, Ella, it's not..." Avery tried to stop her sister.

"A mystery!" Ella declared. "Our Mimi is a mystery writer. It must be in our blood because Avery and I run into mysteries all the time. This inventory list, the grumpy delivery driver, and the missing cookies have mystery written all over them!"

"Are you saying you think Ms. Tara is a cookie thief?" Annie said, mostly joking.

"That's exactly what I'm saying," Ella folded her arms and eyed her friends. "And we're going to catch her."

# 8

## LOTS OF LOOT

The next morning, Ella tried to push her thoughts about the looming mystery aside and focus on selling cookies. She was really proud of their table. The girls had glued cookie shapes to the bright green tablecloth. Taped to the front of the table were their homemade signs listing the cookie names, prices, and how they planned to use the money raised for a good cause.

"This looks awesome, if I do say so myself!" Annie announced. She stood back and admired their work.

"It sure does, ladies! But it's missing just one thing," suggested Mimi. She was the girls' chaperone for the day, along with Kate's mother, Mrs. Dean. Mimi placed a bundle of red balloons at the corner of the table.

"Here's some pizzazz to draw attention," she announced. "Now it's perfect!" Mrs. Dean gave Mimi a thumbs-up in agreement.

"Oooh, our first customer!" Ella exclaimed. "Well, almost our first customer," she added, glancing behind her. Papa sat in a lawn chair nearby, digging into the cookie box he had bought a few minutes earlier. "Mmmm...good cookies," he mumbled between bites.

The girls scrambled behind the table and displayed their biggest smiles. Avery nervously straightened the stacked cookie boxes. She nudged Ella with her elbow. "Go ahead, Ella, try it out," she urged.

"Would you..." Ella's voice sounded squeaky and quiet. She cleared her throat. With more confidence, she tried again. "Would you like to buy some Girl Scout Cookies?"

The woman was older, around Mimi's age. She perked up when she approached the table.

"Hello, girls!" she said cheerfully. Ella was relieved when she saw the woman's kind smile. "I would love to buy some cookies. Two boxes of chocolate mint—that's my favorite. And three boxes of lemon—that's my husband's favorite." She winked at Ella.

"Yes ma'am," Ella said excitedly. "Our cookies are five dollars a box, so your total is twenty-five dollars."

The woman handed her two twenty-dollar bills. Ella felt her face get hot with nerves. She'd never handled much money before, especially someone else's money. Ella propped open the metal change box and quickly did the math in her head. Forty minus twenty-five was fifteen. She grabbed the change and handed it back to the kind lady.

"Thank you, sweetie!" the woman said. "And good luck with your sales. It looks like your money is going to a great cause." The woman strolled her cart into the store with a smile. Just like that, Ella had made her very first cookie sale.

"That felt ahhhmazing!" Ella exclaimed. She gave Annie a high-five.

"You were really good," Annie said, "and you did the math so fast!"

"Thanks!" Ella replied. "It made me nervous to take her money."

"Can't talk now, Ella," Avery interrupted, pointing to several more customers headed toward the entrance.

The girls spent the next couple of hours selling cookies with big smiles and courteous conversation. Luckily, Mrs. Graham arrived with extra boxes.

"They were delivered early this morning," Mrs. Graham said, breathless from carrying boxes of cookies across the parking lot. "They came all the way from the bakery in Virginia!" Ella and Annie exchanged a look.

"Maybe the other factory had to send more boxes because of, you know, the *thief*," Annie whispered.

Ella nodded but didn't comment. It did seem strange that the cookies would come from so far away when there was a factory so close. But she still couldn't figure out why someone would want to steal cookies.

After four straight hours of cookie selling, the girls sold a combined total of 208 boxes. Tired and hot from the midday sun, Avery closed the change box and suggested they break for lunch. Mimi offered to buy the girls some sandwiches from the store deli.

"We agreed to split our sales numbers evenly," Avery said. "So that means we have each sold 52 boxes!" Avery said.

"Wow!" Ella exclaimed. "In one day! I think I might sell *more* than my goal!"

"We are making really good progress," Avery commented. "Let's take a break and grab a..."

Avery stopped talking abruptly.

"Grab a...?" Kate asked.

"A cold drink!" Annie said.

"Better yet, a cold ice cream!" Ella added.

"Shhhhhhh!" Avery waved her hands for the girls to stop talking. "Look!"

A white truck with a pink and green logo pulled into the back of the grocery store parking lot.

"That can't be!" Annie exclaimed.

Ella squinted to see the person climbing out of the truck. The thick legs, blue shirt, and gray hair definitely belonged to Ms. Tara.

"What is she doing here?" Ella whispered.

The girls sat at the table silently as Ms. Tara walked right past them and into the store without looking their way.

"Do you think she remembers us?" Kate asked.

"It's hard to tell," Avery said. "She might not have recognized us."

"Or she might be avoiding us," Ella suggested.

"Suddenly I'm not so hungry anymore," Annie said. The girls nervously waited for Ms. Tara to emerge from the store again.

"We need to keep an eye on her," Ella said. "If she really is a cookie thief, we've got lots of loot right here in the open."

"She's not getting any of these cookies," Annie declared. She jumped in front of the table and spread out her arms in defense.

Finally, Ms. Tara walked out with one plastic bag in her hand. She glanced toward the girls with no reaction. The four girls refused to take their eyes off Ms. Tara until she stepped into her truck and pulled the door shut.

"That woman gives me the creeps," Annie said with a shiver.

"Guys!" Kate carefully crossed the sidewalk, picked something up, and came back to the table.

"What is it?" Avery asked. She impatiently grabbed the paper out of Kate's hand.

1 gallon of milk    $2.99
1 gallon of milk    $2.99

"All she bought was two gallons of milk," Annie said flatly. "I thought she might buy something a little creepier."

"Yeah, but what goes best with milk?" Avery said, cocking her head.

"Cookies!" Ella replied, pointing to the delivery truck. As she drove away, Ms. Tara took a big bite out of a shortbread Girl Scout Cookie.

# 9

# SHORTBREAD SUSPECTS

Annie's mouth dropped open. "Is she really eating a Girl Scout Cookie? How obvious can you be?"

"I just don't understand what she's doing down here," Avery wondered. "Mrs. Graham said her delivery came from a different Girl Scout Cookie bakery in Virginia. That means Ms. Tara didn't have any local deliveries to make today."

"Do you think she was looking for us?" Kate asked.

"Why would she want to find us?" Annie asked.

"Maybe she knows," Ella answered. She felt her stomach flip-flop.

"Knows what?" Avery said. She gave Ella a concerned look.

"Maybe she knows the inventory list is missing. Maybe she knows I took it. Maybe she knows that I know she's lying," Ella said, talking faster and faster. "Maybe she did see us standing here. Maybe she ignored us on purpose. Maybe she thinks we're a threat!"

"Guys...weren't there *five* boxes of cookies here before?" Kate pointed to the table with only two boxes left.

"Yes, those are our display boxes. We've had the same number sitting there all day. Just a minute ago I straightened two boxes of chocolate caramels and three boxes of shortbreads," Avery said.

"Well there are only two boxes of chocolate caramels left," Kate said.

"Wait, we watched her all the way to the car, so there's no way she could have taken them," Ella remarked.

"Do you think...well...I don't know," Annie stumbled and paused.

"It's OK, Annie, what are you thinking?" Ella urged.

"Well, I'm not a good detective or anything," Annie said, "and I've never been part of a mystery. But I was thinking maybe Ms. Tara isn't working alone."

"I think you may be right, Annie," Avery said. "So far we have two clues, a suspect, and more stolen cookies. It wouldn't surprise me at all if there's a whole slew of cookie thieves out there!"

Ella felt a tingle of fear mixed with a thrill of excitement. She was determined to solve this mystery, no matter how big it turned out to be!

# 10

## COOKIE (SELLING) MONSTER

"We have to keep our momentum going!" Avery said. Kate and Annie had come home with Avery and Ella after school. Avery had sold cookies before, but this year felt different, and not just because a mystery was afoot. She was impressed with how many boxes they sold at the Mega Mart and she could hardly hide her excitement to sell more. "I say we do our Cookie Walkabout this week."

"How about tomorrow?" Kate suggested.

"Perfect, we can meet at our house after school," Avery said. "We can go to that new neighborhood we pass on the way to school. I have a friend who lives there. There are lots of houses so I think it would be a good place to sell."

"We'll have to ask Mimi to come with us," Ella added.

"You're right, we have to have a chaperone," Avery said. "I'm sure Mimi wouldn't mind if we bribed her with a big bowl of delicious ice cream as payment!"

"Only if I can have some too!" Annie chirped.

"Since you're Brownies..." Avery started in her familiar know-it-all voice.

"Yeah, yeah, since we're Brownies, we are silly and inexperienced and we can't do anything without help from my big sister Avery," Ella rolled her eyes and giggled.

Avery's face turned red. "If you don't want help, fine." She folded her arms in front of her chest and plopped down on the bed.

"I'm just *kidding*!" Ella said. "Of course we want your advice." Avery folded her arms tighter and turned away.

"Well, I've sold before too, so I'll tell you," Kate jumped in. "First, always stay with the chaperone. Second, never go inside someone's house. Third, always ask if they'd like to buy multiple boxes of cookies."

"Yes, the number one reason why people don't buy cookies is because they weren't asked," Avery blurted out. She couldn't stand not sharing her expertise.

"Right," Kate agreed. "Let's see, what else. Oh! Always wear your vest. And if they aren't ready to purchase cookies right then, make sure you tell them about the Digital Cookie."

"A digital cookie!?" Annie stuck her tongue out and frowned. "What is that—an invisible cookie?"

"You haven't heard of the Digital Cookie?" Kate asked, surprised.

"Not unless I ate it and didn't know it," Annie remarked.

"You don't *eat* it," Avery said, exasperated. "It's an online cookie-selling tool. If you have a customer who wants cookies but doesn't want to buy them right away, you can send them to the Digital Cookie. You give them your personal Digital Cookie website address. They go there and buy as many boxes as they want."

"So that's the link Mrs. Graham handed out a few weeks ago," Ella said. She felt like a light bulb had turned on above her head.

"Duh, what else did you think it was?" Avery asked her sister. She gave Ella a mischievous smile to let her know they were even.

The next afternoon after school, the girls dressed in their Girl Scout vests and hopped in the minivan with Mimi.

"Where should we start, ladies?" Mimi chirped. She was eager to drive the girls around for a big bowl of Rocky Road.

"We have to run by the library," Avery replied. "Mrs. Graham said she would set some boxes in the hallway so we could grab what we need for our sales. I was thinking we could put some in gift bags to put in our wagon. That way people will feel like it's even more of a special treat. I saw some girls do it last year and thought it was a great idea!"

"I like it!" Kate said.

After the girls loaded a tall stack of boxes into the minivan, Avery directed Mimi to the new neighborhood on the way to their school. Rambling houses with cozy front porches, manicured yards, and blooming gardens lined the road.

Mimi pulled the minivan past a row of mailboxes and stopped near the cul-de-sac at the end of the street. "You girls go ahead, I'll follow you with the car." The girls jumped out of the minivan and unloaded their red wagon from the trunk. They filled it with gift bags full of cookie boxes, and pulled the wagon behind them as they headed up the sidewalk.

Avery nudged Ella ahead of her as they approached the front door of the first house. Ella carefully pressed the doorbell button. A young woman carrying a baby cracked the door, smiled, and opened it all the way.

"Hello, my name is Ella and I'm a Girl Scout," Ella said. "We are selling cookies. Are you interested in buying any?"

"I am so glad you stopped by!" the young mom said. Ella noticed her hair was a mess and she had dark circles under her eyes. "I can't get out much with the new baby, but I love Girl Scout Cookies. My favorite kind is the chocolate caramel. Do you have any of those?"

"We sure do! How many boxes would you like?" Ella even impressed herself with how professional she sounded.

"How about three?" the lady replied. She reached for her purse with her free arm.

"Would like any other kinds? Our chocolate mints are popular," Ella suggested.

"Umm, sure," said the first door-to-door customer. "I'll take two chocolate mints as well."

"Perfect!" Ella gave the lady her change, thanked her, and stepped back down the porch stairs to the sidewalk.

Avery was grinning from ear to ear. "What?" Ella asked. "Do I have leftover lunch in my teeth or something?"

"You did really great, Ella," Avery said proudly. "I think you're a natural at this."

Ella suddenly smiled. "I couldn't have

done any of it without your help," she said, and gave Avery a quick, tight squeeze.

"All right, enough mushy stuff. We've got cookies to sell!" Annie declared. She grabbed Ella's arm and pulled her toward the next house.

At first, Ella felt uncomfortable ringing strangers' doorbells. But with the reassurance of Avery, and Mimi waving her on from the minivan, she started to gain confidence. Almost every home had someone who wanted to buy at least one box of cookies. The girls had to keep running back to the minivan to refill their wagon. Ella learned it really was true—people buy more when you just ask!

The sun started to turn golden orange and the shadows on the street pavement stretched long and lazy. The girls had been selling for hours.

"We should get back before the sun sets," Avery remarked. "Plus, Mimi looks a little tired." The girls glanced at the minivan where Mimi gave them a lackluster wave and a half-smile.

"Just one more, Avery. I'm on a selling streak!" Ella pleaded. She gave Avery her best pretty-please-puppy-dog eyes.

"ONE more," Avery agreed. She turned to Kate and whispered, "I think we've created a cookie-selling monster!"

The girls came to a two-story house with white siding. A "For Sale" sign with a large sticker that said "SOLD" was still staked in the yard. Ella confidently stretched out her finger to ring the doorbell.

A middle-aged woman with dark brown eyes and bright red hair opened the door. Ella gasped. Ella hadn't thought about her since that day, but she would recognize the woman's face anywhere. It was the lady who added the wrong ingredient during their bakery tour!

# 11

## SUSPICIOUS ACCOMPLICE

Ella stood with her mouth open until Kate stepped in and took over the sale.

"Hi, we are selling Girl Scout Cookies. Are you interested in buying some?" Kate asked. The woman fiddled with her hands and looked very uncomfortable.

"I think I'm OK," she said quickly. She glanced back at Ella who was still staring, except now her eyes were focused inside the house. Towers of brightly colored cardboard boxes lined the wall behind the door from carpet to ceiling. Ella couldn't see them in detail, but she was sure they were Girl Scout Cookie boxes.

"Did someone from our troop already sell cookies to you?" Ella asked. She couldn't hide the edge in her voice.

"N-no, why?" the woman replied, tripping over her words.

"Oh, no reason, ma'am," Avery said. "We just don't like to bother our customers too much!" Avery gave her a polite smile. "Thank you for your time."

The woman softly closed the door as Avery yanked her sister off the front porch. They walked silently and quickly to the minivan. Avery plopped in her seat, slammed her seatbelt into the lock and turned to her little sister.

"What was THAT?" Avery said in a frantic whisper. She didn't want to yell in front of Mimi. "You were so rude to that woman back there."

"Don't you know who that was?" Ella asked. Avery stared back, confused.

"Avery, that was the woman from the bakery!" Ella exclaimed. "She was the one who added the wrong ingredient to the cookies. Did you even look inside her house?"

"What?" Avery said, annoyed. "I don't peek into people's houses. It's rude, Ella."

"Well, if you had," Ella responded, "you would have seen at least 50, no, maybe 100 boxes of Girl Scout cookies lined up just inside her door."

"What?" Annie asked. She didn't bother to whisper.

"Are you sure, Ella?" Avery said. "Not *everything* is a mystery."

"I'm sure, Avery." Ella nodded her head.

"Wait, Ella, are you saying that..." Kate asked. She started to piece the facts together.

"Yes, that woman from the factory has to be helping Ms. Tara steal the cookies," Ella declared.

"But why would she want to do that? She already made a mistake at her job. Stealing cookies could get her into even more trouble," Avery said.

"Maybe she just bought all those cookies," Annie suggested.

"But she said no one else from our troop tried to sell her cookies yet," Ella said. "How would she already have that many boxes?"

"I just don't know, Ella. It seems like a stretch. You have no proof," Avery said.

"Um...that looks like **blatant** proof to me," Annie remarked, pointing out the minivan window. As Mimi turned right onto the main highway, a white delivery truck turned left into the neighborhood. Avery stretched around to get a glimpse of the driver. Just as she suspected, Ms. Tara had one hand on the steering wheel and one hand holding a shortbread cookie.

"Is that proof enough for you, Avery?" Ella asked sharply.

"If that wasn't, I've got some more for you," Kate added. Her voice sounded uneasy. "I was just looking over our inventory list and we have ten boxes of shortbread cookies unaccounted for."

"You mean we didn't sell them?" Avery asked slowly.

"We didn't sell them," Kate said, "but they're definitely not here."

# 12

# CLUES, NOT COOKIES

"Mimi, we have to go back," Ella blurted out. Avery gave her questioning stare.

"What are you doing?" Avery whispered. Ella ignored her big sister.

"I think we left some extra boxes back at the last house," Ella continued.

"Uh oh, sweetie, I'm all for giving customers a deal, but I don't think we should give cookies away for free!" Mimi said. She looked knowingly at the girls. "And I don't want you getting into more hot water looking for missing boxes like you did in that delivery truck!" Mimi turned the minivan around and headed back down the street. "Let's go get 'em!"

"Ella, we can't go back there!" Avery whispered so Mimi couldn't hear. "Plus, we don't know for sure that the delivery truck was headed to that house. What are you planning to do once we get there?"

"I haven't decided yet," Ella said. "But I know someone took our cookies. Ms. Tara was in the truck. The lady from the factory was in her house. So, there must be another accomplice. If we don't get to the bottom of this soon, we won't have any cookies left to sell!"

Mimi slowly pulled up to the house and parked the minivan. Ella spotted the big white delivery truck parked in the road a few feet from the house. "OK, girls, I'll wait here," Mimi said, and pulled out her phone to text Papa.

"Let's go," Ella urged. The other girls stared back at her.

"Go where?" Annie said. She crawled out of the van and stood by Ella. "Ella, you're my best friend, but I've got to say, this does seem a little crazy."

Kate and Avery reluctantly joined the other girls. "I don't think we're going to find the boxes of cookies," Ella said.

"Sooo, why are we here?" Kate said. She circled her index finger next to her ear to indicate Ella was acting crazy.

"That's not why I wanted to come back," Ella said.

"But you told your Mimi..." Annie started.

"I know, I know. And technically, there are some extra boxes around here," Ella said. "But I really wanted to come back to find clues, not cookies."

"OK, Ella, I'll go with you on this one, but we have to be careful," Avery said. "We can't go in the house, so where do you want to investigate?"

Ella surveyed the scene. The house was off limits. They might be seen snooping around the yard. She turned toward the delivery truck. The front seat was empty.

"There," Ella pointed toward the truck. "There have to be some clues in the truck."

Avery glanced at Mimi who was happily distracted texting Papa. She motioned for the girls to follow her toward the truck. They trotted quickly down the sidewalk and ducked behind the delivery truck's tall wheel well. They didn't want the woman from the factory to see them from her house.

Ella crossed her fingers, reached up, and squeezed the driver door handle. It clicked open easily.

"Unlocked!" Ella whispered. "Yessss!" She crawled up into the truck, being careful to keep her head low. Several boxes of shortbread cookies were strewn along the floor along with empty quart sized cartons of milk.

"Ms. Tara *really* likes her cookies," Ella said.

"She has to. It takes a crazy kind of person to steal from innocent Girl Scouts," Annie said. She was keeping watch on the street while Kate and Avery snuck around the back of the truck.

Ella searched the dashboard and glove box. She found a few receipts for gas and a vehicle registration card, but nothing important to the mystery at hand.

"I don't see anything," Ella said, defeated. "I was sure there would be a clue here."

"What's that?" Annie pointed to piece of trash on the floor. Ella looked closer and saw it was actually a ripped piece of cardboard from a cookie box.

"Trash?" she asked, distracted. She ignored the cardboard and kept looking.

"No, it's got something written on it, on the corner, see?" Annie said. She grabbed the piece of cardboard and held it closely to her face. "It's small writing, but it's there."

"Let me see," Ella said.

Library- 157 boxes
community center - 15 boxes
Mega Mart - 3 boxes
Thrifty Mart - 6 boxes
walkabout - 10 boxes

"What is it?" Annie asked.

Ella read the list over and over again. "I'm not sure," she remarked. "It says boxes, which obviously has to be boxes of cookies. The different places seem like good places to sell cookies."

"Maybe it's a list of how many cookies someone has sold and where," Annie suggested.

"Maybe, but why would Ms. Tara need to sell cookies?" Ella asked. She wasn't convinced. "Let's show Avery."

Ella hopped down from the truck and ran around the back where Avery and Kate sat on the back bumper.

"I think we found something," Ella handed her big sister the list.

"What do you think it means?" Annie asked anxiously.

Avery looked at the list for a few minutes before answering. "I think the cookie thief is keeping track of what she steals and where," Avery said, finally.

"Right!" Ella exclaimed. She was annoyed she hadn't figured it out herself.

"But that's not the most interesting part," Avery added.

"What?" Ella asked. She wondered if she had missed something on the clue.

"I think *our* missing boxes are on the list," Avery said. "Look." She turned the paper so that all three girls could see the writing. "Three boxes taken at the Mega Mart. That's how many shortbreads went missing at the grocery store."

"Ten boxes Walkabout," Kate read. "We were just on our Walkabout sale, and we just realized we have ten missing boxes!"

"Whoa, that's creepy," Annie said. "How would Ms. Tara know, and make a list that quickly? She wasn't even here when we were."

"I don't know," Ella said. She had the uneasy feeling she was being watched.

# 13

# RESTLESS RUN-IN

Suddenly Ella heard the loud stomp of heavy boots getting closer and closer to the back of the truck.

"YOU again!" Ms. Tara boomed.

Avery and Kate, who were sitting on the truck bumper, jumped to their feet.

"What in the world are you girls doing around my truck again?" Ms. Tara snapped. She looked especially frazzled. Her hair was frizzy, her shirt untucked, and dark circles shadowed her eyes.

"We, um, well..." Ella stumbled. She couldn't think of a good reason to tell Ms. Tara. She glanced at her sister. Avery's blue eyes flashed a warning not to say too much!

"We just finished selling cookies and decided to take a break," Annie said. Ella let out a sigh of relief. She hadn't realized she was holding her breath.

"You kids think you can do whatever you want," Ms. Tara lectured. "You can't just plop down on someone's private property. This is *my* truck!"

"We're sorry, we just needed to take a rest," Avery said.

"Did you look in the back?" Ms. Tara said shortly.

"Why? What's in the back?" Ella asked. Her voice was confident and steady.

"Nothing," Ms. Tara quickly responded. "I mean, cookies, of course."

"Oh, just cookies," Ella remarked. She wanted to catch Ms. Tara in a lie. "Where are you taking them?" Ella's voice was sticky sweet.

"I'm headed back to the factory, not that it's any of your business," Ms. Tara said with a scowl.

"Interesting," Ella said under her breath.

"What was that?" Ms. Tara eyed Ella.

"What, uh, I said, uh, yummy things," Ella replied. "Those cookies sure are yummy things!" Ella knew she sounded crazy.

Ms. Tara just rolled her eyes. "I don't have time for a group of little girls interfering with my job. Step away from the truck." Ms. Tara motioned toward the sidewalk, and the girls obeyed her order.

Ms. Tara climbed in the truck. Ella held her breath and hoped she wouldn't notice the piece of cardboard missing from the floor. She clutched the clue in her pocket.

As she drove away, Ms. Tara pointed straight at Ella and stared at her with a menacing look.

"Did you guys see that?" Ella asked.

"She does not look happy with you," Avery said. "We better get out of here before she comes back or we get into more trouble."

The girls raced back to the minivan, relieved to see Mimi's familiar face.

"Find what you needed?" Mimi asked cheerfully.

"I'm not sure," was all Ella could muster. Mimi smiled a kind smile in the rear view mirror and pulled out into the street.

"I'm sorry, Sweetie," Mimi said. "Am I mistaken, or was that the nice lady who saved you from the back of her delivery truck and called me to pick you up?"

"That's her," Ella said flatly. She couldn't understand how Mimi could mistake Ms. Tara for being even remotely nice.

"It's not every day someone takes care of others like that," Mimi said.

Ella was surprised Ms. Tara had Mimi so fooled.

# 14

## OBVIOUS OBSESSION

"I think this whole situation has gotten out of hand," Avery said. The girls were back in Ella's bedroom while Mimi happily ate her ice cream on the couch downstairs.

"Maybe we should tell Mrs. Graham," Annie suggested.

"I agree," Kate said. "This cookie thief is affecting our whole troop."

"I agree too," Avery said. "What do you think, Ella? Ella?"

Ella stared at the wall, her eyes blank.

"ELLA!" Avery yelled.

Ella flinched like she had just woken up. "Huh? Oh, um, what was the question?"

"Is something wrong?" Avery asked.

Ella shrugged. "I just can't stop going over the clues in my head," she replied. "There has to be a third accomplice. But who is it?"

"I can't figure that out, either," Avery said.

"And something Ms. Tara said keeps bothering me," Ella continued. "She said she was going back to the factory."

"But that's where she works," Kate said.

"I know," Ella replied. "But she also said she had cookies in the back of her truck. Why would a delivery truck driver go back to the factory without finishing the deliveries?"

"Good point!" Annie remarked.

"I think there's more to this mystery than just a thief," Ella said.

"I just can't figure out *why*," Avery said.

"Girl Scout Cookies *are* delicious," Annie offered.

"Of course, but anyone can buy them," Avery continued. "Most people are happy to buy them because they know their money goes to a good cause. You don't need cookies to survive, so why steal them?"

"Maybe she likes the thrill of it all," Kate suggested.

"What's thrilling about hoarding cardboard boxes?" Ella asked.

"I just think she likes the cookies," Annie said. "You should have seen the inside of her truck. There were empty shortbread boxes everywhere. Plus, every time we see her she's eating a shortbread cookie. I think she's addicted!"

"Wait," Avery said. "Did you see any other kinds of cookie boxes in her truck?"

"No," Annie said. "They were definitely all shortbread boxes because I remember thinking she must be obsessed."

"That's something!" Avery declared. "Now we know she isn't just stealing Girl Scout cookies. She's stealing one kind of cookie—shortbreads."

Ella pulled the piece of cardboard she found in the truck from her pocket. "So she took 157 boxes from the library. That had to be the night of the cookie-selling meeting when Mrs. Graham didn't have enough boxes."

"Those were probably the boxes you saw in the back of her truck!" Annie said.

"It had to be," Ella continued down the list. "The three boxes from the Mega Mart and the ten boxes from the Cookie Walkabout sale makes perfect sense. That was us. We just don't know who stole them."

"Someone's sneaky and fast!" Kate said.

"But I can't figure out the Community Center and the Thrifty Mart," Ella looked the list over one more time.

"It must mean she's stolen boxes from other girls in our troop," Avery said. "I heard Emily mention trying to sell at the Thrifty Mart."

"I bet she's stealing boxes from everyone!" Ella said.

"I wonder if anyone else has noticed any missing inventory," Kate said.

"That's why we have to tell Mrs. Graham," Avery said again. "We all agree. Ella, what do you think?"

Ella wasn't sure she wanted to involve someone else in the mystery, but she was beginning to feel like she was in over her head.

"We should tell her," Ella said finally.

"Agreed," Avery declared. "We'll do it at our next meeting." Avery grabbed her sister's hand and gave it a gentle squeeze. Ella wanted to feel better, but she knew she wouldn't feel comfortable again until the mystery was solved.

# 15

# COOKIE COUNT CONUNDRUM

It was almost a week until the next troop meeting and Ella could hardly stand the wait. Finally, Monday afternoon rolled around. Ella burst through the doors to the library ten minutes before the meeting was scheduled to start. She and Avery explained the situation to Mrs. Graham who decided to take inventory of each girl's sales just as a precaution.

"Good evening, ladies! Tonight we are going to celebrate our progress!" Mrs. Graham winked at Avery and Ella. She always had a way of putting a positive spin on things. "I'd like each of you to stand up and tell us how many boxes you have sold and how many you have left. We'll start right here in the front."

Riley stood up and proudly announced she'd sold 42 boxes and had 58 left. One by one, each girl stood up and described their progress. Mrs. Graham recorded each number on a small notepad. As the last girl sat down, Mrs. Graham looked concerned. She hunched over her notebook, her lips moving as she added up the lines of numbers.

"This stinks! If cookies keep disappearing, I'll never reach my goal of selling 200 boxes," Ella said.

"And my sister and other handicapped people will never get their ramp," Annie said.

While they were waiting, a tall girl with red hair approached Mrs. Graham's folding table at the front of the room. Ella strained to hear Mrs. Graham's conversation with the girl. She could only get bits and pieces. The redhead's words were, "you didn't count...I've sold...300 and...I have 200...boxes left."

"Did you hear that?" Ella whispered to Annie. "That girl said she's sold 300 boxes. Three HUNDRED! How in the world has she sold so many? And I heard her say she has 200 left!"

"Who is that?" Annie squinted to see across the room.

"I don't know, she must be new in the troop," Ella said. "We've got to tell Avery."

Ella and Annie scooted back a few rows to two empty seats by Avery and Kate. Ella filled in her big sister on the redhead's sales.

"Are you sure you heard right, Ella?" Avery asked. "Those numbers seem off. Mrs. Graham hasn't given any Girl Scouts 500 boxes of cookies. That seems like way too many."

"Only one way to find out," Kate said. Ella looked at her, confused. "We ask her," Kate announced.

The girls quieted as Mrs. Graham stood up from her table.

"Well, ladies, we have a small discrepancy in our inventory numbers," she explained. "I need all of you to make sure you keep good track of your sales. That way, we know exactly how many boxes you've sold and how many you have left. We are trying very hard to reach our goal so we can buy supplies to build a handicap ramp to help Annie's sister and other handicapped citizens in our town for our Bronze Award Project. You are all doing a great job and I am very proud of your hard work!"

Mrs. Graham continued with the rest of meeting. Ella tapped her foot against the floor until the meeting ended. She knew she had to approach the new girl, but she wasn't sure what to say.

When Mrs. Graham dismissed the girls, Ella slowly made her way to the back of the room where the new girl still sat in her chair.

"Hi, my name is Ella," Ella stretched out her hand toward the new girl. She shook it once.

"I'm Julia," she said softly.

"I haven't seen you here before," Ella said. "Are you new?"

"I just moved here," Julia said. "My mom was a Girl Scout growing up. She thought I might make some friends in the local troop."

"Well, it seems like you've adjusted really well," Ella remarked. "I mean, you've sold more cookies than any other girl here." Ella tried to keep her voice calm and polite.

"Oh, you heard." Julia shuffled her feet on the floor and twisted in her seat.

"Yeah, 300 boxes! That's incredible!" Ella said.

"I actually sold 326," Julia said, almost mechanically. "Not that it matters," she quickly corrected. "I'm just trying to keep good inventory like Mrs. Graham said."

Ella thought Julia seemed uncomfortable.

"Wow, how did you sell so many?" Ella asked. We didn't have 300 boxes to sell even if we wanted to!"

"Oh, well, I, uh..." Julia stalled. "I just sell what I have," she said quickly.

Julia grabbed her bag off the floor, quickly stood up and told Ella goodbye.

"It was nice to meet you," Ella said. Julia only nodded her head as she walked out the door.

Avery walked up to Ella. "What did she say?" she asked.

"Not much," Ella replied. "Just that she only sold the cookies she had."

"But Mrs. Graham hasn't given anyone that many cookies," Avery said.

"Maybe she's getting them from someone else," Kate joined in. "Look!" She pointed to a small piece of folded paper on the floor. "Maybe you guys have rubbed off on me, but I have a feeling that's more than just a piece of trash."

Ella reached down and unfolded the paper.

128 oakwood Trail
SWTTRT123

"That has to be an address," Annie said.

"And that's the code the lady from the Sweet Treat factory told us about, the one that's on every box of Girl Scout cookies they bake," Avery said.

"That has to be where Julia is getting her extra cookies!" Annie said.

"If that's where she's getting her extra cookies—ones that Mrs. Graham didn't give her—that means one thing," Ella reasoned. "She has to be getting them from the cookie thief. And now we know exactly where the thief lives!" Ella smiled, but felt a tingle of fear creep down her spine.

# 16

## SERIOUS STRATEGY

After several days, the girls had a plan. They knew they couldn't just show up at a thief's house without a serious strategy.

"OK, let's go through it one more time," Avery said. All four girls were huddled under a multicolored quilt in Avery and Ella's living room. Annie and Kate were spending the night again. The only light in the room was the streaming beam of the full moon through the window. The next day was Saturday.

"Time?" Avery asked.

"We pull out at 10:00 a.m. sharp," Ella answered.

"Check. Chaperone?" Avery said.

"Mimi," Annie offered.

"Check. Supplies?"

"Girl Scout uniform. Cell phone. Cookie boxes," Kate said automatically.

"Annnnnd..." Avery peered through the dim light under the quilt.

"Oh, and cookie dough ice cream for Mimi!" Kate added.

"Check. The plan?"

"We approach the address carefully," Ella said. "We don't go inside. We present our accusation, and wait for their reaction. If they confess, we call the police. If they resist, we play it safe, leave with Mimi, and tell Mrs. Graham," Ella recited.

"Check," Avery said. "I think we're ready! Let's catch a thief!"

Ella tossed and turned all night in her sleeping bag on the living room floor. Avery seemed to have all the details planned, but Ella still felt unprepared. What would she say? What would the cookie thief do? What if her detective instincts had been wrong all along?

Finally, dapples of sunlight flittered over the wood floor as the sun began to rise. Ella got up early, took her shower, and went over the plan again and again in her head. Sometimes she wished she could tell Mimi about the mystery to get her advice, but she knew Mimi wouldn't want her to get involved. Ella had to solve this mystery, and she couldn't stop now.

The girls piled in the "Mimi-van" at 10:00 sharp.

"We are planning to sell lots of cookies today," Avery said cheerily to Mimi. "But first, we have to go by this address." Avery typed 128 Oakwood Trail into the minivan's GPS. "I'm not sure where it is, so I'll tell you where to turn."

"OK, sweetie, but nobody likes a back seat driver!" Mimi chuckled at her joke. Ella's stomach was in too many knots to laugh at anything. She felt her palms get sweaty as they pulled out of the driveway.

Avery directed Mimi to turn on the main road outside of their neighborhood. After a few more turns, the houses started to look very familiar.

"I thought you already sold cookies here, Avery," Mimi said.

"Um, take one more right," Avery said. Mimi turned on the same street where they sold cookies door-to-door just days before.

"Avery?" Ella looked at her sister with concern in her eyes. Avery just shook her head, clearly confused.

"Here we are, 128 Oakwood Trail," Mimi announced.

Avery gasped. Annie's mouth fell open.

Ella recognized the house right away. It was unmistakable. The "For Sale" sign was still staked in the front yard and a big white delivery truck sat in the driveway.

# 17

## SUSPECT SURPRISE!

"Are you guys sure we should do this?" Annie said. "Maybe it isn't worth it. We don't know what will happen when we ring that doorbell."

"Mimi is here," Avery said. "She won't let anything happen. We will follow the safety precaution rules. We will be smart and careful."

"We have to, Annie," Ella grabbed her friend's hands and gave her a reassuring look. "If you don't want to come with us, you can stay in the car."

"Ladies? Are you getting out?" Mimi was unaware of the drama in the back seat.

"No, we're in this together," Annie decided.

"Let's do this!" Kate said. The girls climbed out of the van and slowly walked up the sidewalk. Ella spotted a box of open shortbread cookies through the passenger window of the delivery truck.

"It has to be Ms. Tara," Avery said. "I can't say that I'm surprised."

"And her accomplice is definitely the woman from the factory," Kate stated. "It makes sense now. They were working together all along. That's why Ella saw all the boxes stacked in the living room. I'm sure we'll see them as soon as she opens the door."

"OK, remember the plan," Avery said. "We know Ms. Tara can be stern. And we certainly aren't sure how she will react to our accusation."

Ella stepped on the porch and boldly walked to the front door. She stuck her finger out and, after a moment of hesitation, pushed the doorbell button.

The girls heard the chime of the bell and footsteps just inside the door. They looked at each other, concern reflecting in all of their eyes.

"Can I help you?" the soft voice didn't sound like Ms. Tara or the woman from the factory. As she cracked the door, a tendril of red hair fell over the girl's shoulder.

"Julia???" Ella asked. She couldn't believe her eyes.

# 18

# RING OF THIEVES

Julia stared back at the girls. Ella couldn't decide if she looked embarrassed or upset.

"Hi Ella," Julia almost whispered. "How did you find my house?"

"*Your* house?" Annie said.

"Yes, I live here," Julia said, confused.

"Is that your delivery truck too?" Ella said. There was an unfriendly edge in her voice. Avery looked at her sister and mouthed silently, "Stay calm."

"No, that's Tara's," the name rolled easily off of Julia's tongue.

"Those must be all your cookie boxes there," Ella said. She pointed past Julia into the living room where cookie boxes were stacked. Julia closed the door tighter.

"That's not really your concern," Julia said. "Why are you here?"

"Because it *is* our concern," Ella replied. "You stole our cookies and we are here to claim them!"

"Ella!" Avery said sternly. "I'm sorry, Julia, what my little sister means is this situation looks very suspicious to us."

"How?" Julia's voice grew louder with frustration. "You came to my house. You knocked on my door. You accused me of stealing. It doesn't make any sense. I don't see any suspicion here other than *I'm* suspicious of why *you* are standing on my front porch."

"Let me explain," Avery said calmly. "We have had several cookie boxes go missing. Every time a box has disappeared, we've seen Ms. Tara or her delivery truck. Then we sold cookies here last week. We knocked on this very door and an older woman answered. Ella recognized the woman from our bakery tour and saw the cookie boxes stacked in the living room. The woman acted uncomfortable when Ella asked about them."

Julia shifted her weight to the other foot. "And...?" she asked.

Avery continued. "On our way home, we saw Ms. Tara's delivery truck pulling into the neighborhood. We came back to investigate and found a note in the delivery truck with a list of boxes that had gone missing along with their locations. We concluded that the two women had to be working together to steal our Girl Scout cookies. And we think they might have another accomplice! So when you answered the door this morning, we had to assume you were part of the ring of thieves."

"Ring of thieves?" Julia looked shocked. "No, no. You guys have got this totally wrong!" As Julia was talking, the woman from the factory walked up behind her. Ella recognized the same brown eyes and dark red hair as Julia had.

"Is there a problem, Julia?" the woman asked.

"I don't think so," Julia answered, without looking back at the woman. "All of you, meet my mom."

"Your mom?" Ella asked.

"OK," Annie said. "I'm officially confused."

"This is my mother, Susan," Julia said.

"AND this is the woman from the factory," Ella declared. She couldn't believe the twist of events. "I saw her add chocolate chips to the shortbread recipe. She botched the batch."

"Oh, you saw that?" Susan looked embarrassed. "It was my first week at the factory. I was so nervous."

"Mom, you don't have to explain anything to them," Julia said. "I knew I wouldn't make friends here." Julia's eyes filled with tears.

Ella felt a twinge of guilt.

"I'm sorry, Julia," Ella said. "I'm just confused."

Julia wiped her eyes with the back of her hand. "My mom and I moved here so she could start work at the new factory. What you saw that day was a simple mistake."

Julia explained. "My mom added a wrong ingredient and somehow the cookies got out of the factory. She risked losing her job. We were so afraid because Mom had just bought this house. My mom talked to her boss and asked what she could do to fix her mistake. Her boss told her she had to recover every single box of the wrong shortbread cookies and return them to the factory. Tara has been a huge help in doing that!"

Julia opened the door far enough for the girls to peek in the living room. Ms. Tara sat on the couch in her Sweet Treat uniform watching television.

"She's been driving back and forth from the factory," Julia continued, "to pick up boxes of bad shortbread cookies and take them back." She looked at Ms. Tara and smiled. "We reward her by letting her watch our cable TV. She only gets four channels at her house!"

Ella shook her head. "So, Ms. Tara has been *helping* you?" she asked. Maybe Mimi hadn't been so wrong, after all!

"Yes, she takes our botched boxes and replaces them with a good batch of shortbread cookies," Julia explained. "My mom probably would have lost her job if it weren't for Ms. Tara."

"But I still don't understand," Avery said. "We know we have missing cookie boxes. Mrs. Graham said other girls' boxes have gone missing too. If it's not you, who is the cookie thief?"

"Well, technically, it's me," Julia confessed.

# 19

# CHOCOLATE-Y-CHIPPY MYSTERY

The sun rose high as the day wore on. Mimi sat in the minivan, still **immersed** in the thick book she was reading. Once in a while, she glanced up at Ella and winked. Ella had a feeling Mimi knew about the mystery all along.

The morning had not gone at all how Ella planned. She was sitting on the front porch of the factory woman's house, looking at the white delivery truck in the driveway, talking to the cookie thief—and she wasn't scared at all. In fact, she was starting to like Julia.

"I had to take the boxes," Julia explained. "I went through them quickly before my first Girl Scout meeting when Mrs. Graham was going to pass them out. I found all the shortbreads that were marked SWTTRT123 and dated the day my mother added the chocolate chips. Ms. Tara met me at the library that night to load up the bad cookies and replace them with new boxes."

"Let me guess, you took exactly 157 boxes," Ella said.

"Yes," Julia said. She looked confused. "How did you know?"

"It doesn't matter," Ella said. She and Avery exchanged a smile.

"Mrs. Graham was supposed to have all the cookies she needed," Julia said. "Ms. Tara was going to deliver the bad cookies and get replacements before the meeting was over. But her delivery got held up somehow."

Ella and Annie exchanged an embarrassed look. Ella shivered at the memory of a "rat" tail wrapping around her leg.

"I think we already know about that," Avery said. Julia looked confused but Avery didn't offer to explain.

"I also took the boxes at the grocery store," Julia continued. "I spotted the code on the bottom of three of the boxes on the table. I grabbed them quickly when you weren't looking."

"Oh, we were too busy staring down Ms. Tara," Kate said. "We thought she had an accomplice. At least we were right about one thing!" Kate giggled at the memory.

"I also grabbed the boxes when you rang the doorbell last week," Julia continued. "I was home, but I didn't want you to see me. I snuck around the house and grabbed the bad boxes out of your wagon."

Ella shook her head again. There was a lot to absorb here!

"I called Tara and told her I had 10 more boxes," Julia said. "She was just down the road so she came that night and exchanged the boxes. I wanted to give the boxes back to you, but I didn't have the chance."

"That explains why we saw the delivery truck that day!" Avery exclaimed.

"Man, you're quick!" Annie said.

"And sneaky!" Ella added.

"I guess," Julia replied. "But I planned to replace every box with a good one." Julia looked sincere. "Then you guys had Mrs. Graham count inventory. I knew once she had the numbers from all the girls it would look suspicious if boxes started to show up in surplus. I decided to just keep the good boxes and try to sell them myself."

"So that's how you had 500 boxes," Avery said. "Of course!"

"But I don't understand," Ella said. "Why didn't you just tell us?"

Julia looked embarrassed. "Honestly? I wanted you guys to like me. I didn't want you to know my mom had messed up a batch of Girl Scout cookies. I didn't want you to think I had ruined the cookie-selling season. I don't really have any friends and I didn't want to ruin my chance at making some." Julia looked like she might cry again.

"Well, we're your friends now," Ella announced. "And we'll help you sell as many cookies as you need us to!"

Julia smiled and gave Ella a big hug.

"This has been a really hard month," Julia confessed. "I've really needed a friend. Thank you!"

Ella smiled back at her. She couldn't believe how wrong she'd been about the whole situation.

"Here," Julia handed Ella a shortbread cookie with little black dots speckled in. "Try a 'bad' cookie. They're actually pretty good!"

Ella took a bite of the chocolate chip shortbread.

"Yum! You're right!" Ella said. "Maybe your mom was onto something." Ella laughed. "We could propose a new Girl Scout cookie flavor. We could call it the Chocolate-y-Chippy Mystery Cookie!"

# 20

## SLEEPOVER STRATEGY

That night, Avery and Ella invited Julia to join their sleepover group. All five girls stayed up way too late painting each other's toenails and eating lots of junk food.

"I'm so glad your Mimi bought some boxes of cookies from you two," Kate said. "Selling all these Girl Scout Cookies made me want to eat them so bad!" Kate stuffed a whole chocolate mint cookie into her mouth. The girls giggled at her chocolate-stained teeth.

"I think this is the first time I've relaxed in weeks!" Ella said. "Who knew I'd be so happy with a cookie thief sitting in my own living room?!" Ella winked at Julia, who was busy brushing bright purple nail polish onto her toes.

"I haven't had this much fun in, well, too long to remember," Julia said. "You guys are the best!"

Ella couldn't believe how naturally Julia fit into their group of friends. She was kind, smart, and kept right up with the other girls' silliness.

"I just wish we'd become friends sooner!" Avery said. "For Brownies, you three aren't too terrible to hang out with." Avery smiled at Ella.

"But we do have some work to do," Kate said.

"Always the business leader!" Annie remarked.

"Well, someone has to!" Kate said. "We need to make a plan to sell the rest of Julia's cookies. She has a little more than 200 boxes to sell. I think we can do it!"

"Do you think we'll meet our goal if we sell all the boxes?" Annie asked.

"I've been keeping track of all of our inventory and sales," Kate said. "By my calculations, we won't only meet our individual and group goals, we'll exceed them!"

Ella was excited. She might have the chance to sell over 200 boxes of Girl Scout Cookies in her very first cookie-selling season!

"You guys don't understand how excited my sister will be to get a wheelchair ramp!" Annie said. "This has been the best cookie-selling season EVER!"

"Annie, this has been your *only* cookie-selling season ever," Avery laughed. "But compared to my past ones, it has been pretty great!"

"I think we should sell at the Mega Mart again," Kate said. "We made the most profit there."

"Perfect!" Avery said.

"And this time we don't have to be distracted with looking for a thief!" Ella added. Julia gave her a high-five and smiled.

"I think the best business strategy would be to place tables on either side of the front entrance with two girls at each table," Kate said. "And now that we have five girls, we can add a new level of selling by using the Digital Cookie App."

"I think Annie and I should be at one table," Avery suggested. "Julia and Kate could be at the other. Ella, would you feel comfortable selling with the app?"

"Me?" Ella was surprised.

"Yes, I've been watching you and you've done a great job with the customers. I think you have a knack for it," Avery said.

"Well, if you think so," Ella said, hesitant. "Well, OK."

"Now we just have to find a time that your Mimi and my mom can chaperone," Kate said.

"That shouldn't be a problem for Mimi," Ella said. "My mother just picked up a fresh quart of Rocky Road at the grocery store!" All five girls giggled.

"Your Mimi sounds pretty interesting," Julia said.

"Oh, you have no idea!" Ella replied.

# 21

## SET UP TO SELL

The girls convinced Mimi to spend her Sunday afternoon at the cookie booth outside the grocery store. They donned their uniforms, loaded up their cookies, and set up to sell. Mrs. Dean agreed to meet them there.

They had made a new sign for the front of their table that said, "Girl Scout Cookies—Last Chance!" Avery thought it was a good idea to remind shoppers that Girl Scout Cookie season was almost over!

Ella stood near the door with Mimi's tablet computer. She offered online sales to anyone who didn't want to wait in line. Customers scrolled through different cookie options and selected the boxes they wanted with the touch of their finger. They paid by swiping a credit card on a special device attached to the tablet.

"Well, that was easy," said a mom with three little blond boys. "Who knew the Girl Scouts were so tech savvy?!"

Ella lost track of her digital sales, but she knew she hadn't stopped selling since lunchtime and now the sun hung low in the sky.

"No thank you, I can't have sugar," said one of Avery's customers, politely declining to buy any Girl Scout Cookies. Ella overhead the conversation.

"That's OK!" Ella ran over to the table and interrupted before Avery could respond to the elderly woman wearing a bright pink silk shirt. "If you'd like to," Ella offered, "you could buy a box to donate to our military troops overseas."

"Really?" The lady seemed surprised, but pleased.

"Yes ma'am," Ella said. "Some people can't have sugar or are on a diet. This way they can still buy cookies, but instead of eating the cookies, they get shipped to servicemembers in other countries."

"Isn't that great?! I had no idea," the lady said. "I would love to buy some cookies for our brave troops. I'll buy 10 boxes."

"Wow! Thank you!" Avery said with a huge smile. She accepted the lady's money and wrote her order on a special donation list.

Soon, all the girls' cookie boxes were gone.

"Thank you so much!" Julia said to her new friends. "I didn't know how I was going to sell all those cookies!"

"Sometimes it just takes a little teamwork," Ella declared. She pulled her friends into a group hug. "You guys are awesome!"

# 22

## BURSTING WITH BADGES

A few months later, Ella woke up early, excited about the day's award ceremony. She pulled on freshly pressed khaki pants and a white button-down shirt. She carefully slipped her arms through her Girl Scout vest. There was one empty space left on her first row of badges and she hoped to fill it today.

"Ready?" Avery peeked in Ella's room.

"I think so," Ella said. "Is it weird that I'm nervous?"

"Not at all," Avery reassured her. "Don't tell anyone, but sometimes I still get nervous at these ceremonies."

Mimi and Papa drove Avery and Ella to the local park and parked in a gravel parking lot. There, on a gentle hill overlooking a tree-lined lake, was the white gazebo. Several Girl Scouts and their parents were already sitting in the first row of white plastic chairs. A reporter from the local newspaper chatted with them.

"We couldn't have asked for a prettier day!" Mimi said. Sun sparkled off the lake's deep blue water. Ella thought the freshly painted white gazebo looked more beautiful than ever.

Avery and Ella walked up the hill and found a seat next to Annie, Kate, and Julia. Annie wore a big smile.

"Meet my sister Lacey," Annie said proudly. Lacey shared Annie's long, silky dark hair and olive skin. She sat in a motorized wheelchair.

"So nice to finally meet you," Avery said.

"Welcome!" Mrs. Graham's voice quieted the girls. "We have had an excellent cookie-selling season this year! Not only did we meet our goal, we exceeded it!" The girls applauded and cheered.

"The proceeds you earned from selling cookies this season have been used to pay for the supplies for two things," Mrs. Graham announced. "This new ramp for handicapped citizens is the first thing," she said. "The second thing is a paved sidewalk from the parking lot up the hill!" Cheers broke out again.

"Let me explain how extraordinary this troop is," Mrs. Graham said, addressing the parents, friends, and families in the audience. "Our troop decided to make this gazebo handicap accessible as their project for the Bronze Award. They saw a real need and had a great idea. All we needed to complete our project was some way to buy supplies. The girls worked very hard to sell cookies this season to pay for those supplies."

Mrs. Graham turned toward the wheelchair ramp. "Once the supplies were purchased, the girls helped during the building process, too," she added. "Because these girls worked hard individually *and* as a team to complete this project, I am proud to present the Bronze Award to all the Junior Girl Scouts in my troop!"

Mrs. Graham was beaming. Ella thought she saw tears glistening in her eyes.

"That's the highest Girl Scout award for a Junior!" Avery exclaimed. "I can't believe it!" She couldn't help but jump up and down in excitement.

"That's awesome!" Annie added. "I am so excited about the sidewalk and ramp too. We're going to come here all the time, Lacey!" She squeezed her little sister's hand.

"Now, onto the badge ceremony," Mrs. Graham said. She began to call names and hand out badges to eager Girl Scouts. Each name was met with a round of applause.

"Now," Mrs. Graham continued, "it's time to recognize a special group of sellers. These girls sold more cookies than any other team this year. Ella, Avery, Kate, Annie, and Julia, would you please join me?" Mrs. Graham motioned for the girls to stand next to her in front of the group.

"You have all certainly earned your Cookie Activity Pin for outstanding participation in this cookie-selling season!" Mrs. Graham announced. She smiled at each girl as she handed out the pins. Mrs. Graham turned to the audience again.

"This group of girls worked very hard this year," she added. "They exemplified two important parts of the Girl Scout Law: 'Be a Sister to Every Scout' and 'Be Friendly and Helpful.' When Julia was new and alone, Avery, Kate, Annie, and Ella became sisters to their fellow Girl Scout. And when Julia found herself in need, these girls came together. They were especially friendly and helpful by selling the rest of her cookies as a team. That's why I am so proud to present this group of girls with their special awards."

Mrs. Graham sipped a bottle of water and cleared her throat. "First up," she said, "are my Juniors. Avery and Kate have earned the Cookie CEO Badge!" She approached Avery and Kate with the brightly colored round badge in hand.

Mrs. Graham smiled. "Avery, you showed excellent skills as a Junior seller this year. You especially excelled in meeting and understanding customers as well as making the selling experience pleasant for everyone you met. You learned to make a good impression on all your customers!"

Avery accepted the badge with a big smile.

"Kate," Mrs. Graham continued, "you showed extraordinary skill in managing the inventory and money related to the cookie-selling process. You managed your cookie selling like a successful business!" Kate smiled and nodded at Avery.

"Now, for my sweet Brownies," Mrs. Graham said. She eyed the audience mischievously. "And yes, that pun was intended." The audience chuckled. "This year, my Brownies have worked hard to earn their Meet My Customers Badge!"

She turned to Julia first. "Julia, I'm so proud to have you as part of our troop," Mrs. Graham remarked. "I present your very first Girl Scout badge. Wear it proudly because you earned it!" Julia took the badge from Mrs. Graham and held it like it was a precious gem. "Thank you!" she said. "My mom will be so proud!"

Mrs. Graham turned to Annie. "Your cheerful attitude was important in creating a good customer experience. I saw several occasions when your customers left smiling just because they met you!"

Annie surprised Mrs. Graham with a big hug.

"And last but not least," Mrs. Graham added, motioning to Ella. "Ella, you met and exceeded your personal goal. You approached new customers even when it felt uncomfortable. You worked hard to learn all the 'ins and outs' of what makes a successful cookie sale. I am proud of the job you did this season!"

Ella grinned broadly as she accepted the triangle-shaped badge. It would fit perfectly on her vest!

"Congratulations, ladies!" Mrs. Graham said. "Would any of you like to say something?"

The girls looked at each other and hesitated until Ella blurted out, "Just that I can't wait until next year!"

# The End

# About the Author

 Carole Marsh is the Founder and CEO of Gallopade International, an award-winning, woman-owned family business founded in 1979 that publishes books and other materials intended to guide, inspire, and inform children of all ages. Marsh is best known for her children's mystery series called **Real Kids! Real Places! America's National Mystery Book Series.**

During her 30 years as a children's author, Marsh has been honored with several recognitions including Georgia Author of the Year and Communicator of the Year. She has also received the iParenting Award for Greatest Products, the Excellence in Education Award, and been honored for Best Family Books by *Learning* Magazine. She is also the author of *Mary America, First Girl President of the United States,* winner of the 2012 Teacher's Choice Award for the Family from *Learning* Magazine.

For more information about Carole Marsh and Gallopade International, please visit www.gallopade.com.

# TALK ABOUT IT!

1. In the beginning of the book, Ella feels embarrassed that she and Annie dressed up when Avery and Kate did not. Ella eventually decides to be confident and enjoy her costume. Can you describe a time when you decided to be confident about a decision you made even when others did not agree with you?

2. At the cookie rally, Mrs. Graham encourages all of the Girl Scouts to review cookie sales techniques and rules, even if they've sold cookies before. Why is good to review techniques and rules even if you think you already know them?

3. Mrs. Graham asks Ella what her personal cookie-selling goals are. Ella sets a high standard to sell 200 boxes. Explain why

goals are important. How can goals help you accomplish new and challenging things?

4. Ella feels nervous when she handles someone else's money for the first time. Have you ever had to accept, count, and make change for someone else? What skills are important to remember when handling money?

5. The girls are careful to follow Girl Scout safety rules for selling cookies, especially on the Cookie Walkabout. Explain why selling in a group, having a chaperone, and wearing the Girl Scout uniform helps to make cookie selling safer.

6. Julia confesses that she doesn't have many friends and is going through several life changes like moving and attending a new Girl Scout Troop. Describe a time when you went through a big change in your life. How did friends help you through the challenging time?

# BRING IT TO LIFE!

*Book Club Activities for a Class or Girl Scout Troop*

1. Everyone has a favorite Girl Scout Cookie. Use your favorite flavor in a new way. Create a recipe incorporating Girl Scout Cookies. Have a tasting party with your friends!

2. Create your own Cookie Kick-Off Parade costume. You can use cardboard boxes as skirts or cut out pictures of cookies to wear, like in the book. Other ideas include colorful streamers, cookie-shaped signs, and custom-decorated chef hats. Be creative!

3. Create your own "cookie-selling" booth. Your product can be anything from bake sale items to a lemonade stand. Decorate your table—be sure to make

signs describing the items for sale and the price of the items. Conduct a mock (or real) sale of your product with your family, friends, or classmates.

4. Create a map of your town. Identify the best spots to sell cookies. Collaborate with friends to come up with a cookie-selling strategy around your town.

5. What cause would you like to donate cookie sale money to? Write a proposal including a description of your idea, why it is important, who will benefit from it, and how much it will cost.

6. Create an inventory list like the one Kate keeps throughout the book. Find your favorite snacks and tally how much of each item is left in your pantry. Watch the item and keep track as the inventory decreases. Use your inventory list to determine when you will need to restock the snack.

# SCAVENGER HUNT

Let's go on a Scavenger Hunt! See if you can find the items below related to the mystery, and then write the page number where you found each one. *(Teachers and Girl Scout Leaders: You have permission to reproduce this page for your students/Girl Scouts.)*

_____ 1.  red balloons

_____ 2.  a vehicle registration card

_____ 3.  Rocky Road ice cream

_____ 4.  polka-dotted socks

_____ 5.  a red wagon

_____ 6.  a wet mop

_____ 7.  chicken nuggets

_____ 8.  purple nail polish

_____ 9.  a gold button with a red ribbon

_____ 10. a newspaper reporter

# SAT GLOSSARY

**abrupt:** sudden and unexpected

**blatant:** completely obvious

**fiasco:** a thing that is a complete failure, especially in a ridiculous or humiliating way

**immersed:** involved deeply in a particular activity or interest

**mishap:** an unlucky accident

*Enjoy this exciting excerpt from:*

# COLUMBIA LASTNAME

## FIRST GIRL COLONIST ON MARS

## by Carole Marsh

# Prologue—Part I
# Before Time Burped

I was born and live in the small, colonial-era port town of Bath, North Carolina. The pirate known as Blackbeard once lived here. It is a pretty little town on a peninsula that juts out into the broad and blue Pamlico River. This river flows out to the Pamlico Sound. Once it reaches the Outer Banks, it sort of snakes its way around all those sandy barrier islands into the Atlantic Ocean.

My friends and I spend lots of time boating on the river and in the creeks...dangling raw chicken pieces off lines of string to catch crabs...or hanging in hammocks reading books.

I live in a building that had been the old colonial library, which has a cool spiral staircase. When I was younger, I could skip all the steps and slide down the center post like it was a fire pole. There are churches and gardens, white picket fences, a tiny Bath post office, and the school.

My parents like to keep a "low profile," they say, in spite of their very-important-and-somewhat-dangerous jobs with NASA, the National Aeronautics and Space Administration, and CITCOS, Citizens of the Cosmos. Except for their jobs, some expensive electronic gadgetry in our home, and the fact that Dad always wanted me to grow up and "move to Mars" (and he wasn't kidding!), my life was just as normal as any other kid's.  *Until...*

Until the day "time burped"—at least that's what my dad called the brief tear in the space-time continuum. That's physics talk. My father is... was? a pretty famous physicist.  But this day changed everything.  He vanished—into a time warp? Another dimension?  For all I know, he went to Disney World?!

Just kidding!

## Prologue—Part II

It was a normal, hot August day. The cicadas *clacked-clacked-clacked* by day, and the katydids *katched-katched-katched* at night.  It made it hard to sleep, up on my rooftop perch beside the sort-of-secret satellite dish and Dad's powerful telescope. I was up there laying on my back on the warm asphalt roof, watching for falling stars—it was the time of the annual Perseid meteor shower.

"Whoa! There goes one!" I said to my dog, Scram.

Dad was down in the family room, glued to some stupid television show for a rare change. Mom was up in their bedroom, reading a mystery book.

I was so busy counting stars that I did not even realize what had happened. There was no screeching sound, no flashing lights, nothing. I didn't even know anything had happened until the following day, actually.

I just went to bed. But the next morning, Dad had vanished, the TV still flickering and his lemonade all melted and sticky on the table. When Mom and I looked around, we realized that nothing else was gone, not his briefcase or papers or computer.

Bath was such an old town in an old farming and fishing community that you couldn't tell by looking at the listing-to-starboard tobacco barns, or the local feed and seed store, or anything else, that sometime in the night, "time had burped."

But Mom knew; she figured it out right away. She sent out a few s-posts (spaceposts, what you might have called e-mail way back when), and then she did something extraordinary: she changed my name.

"Why?" I asked.

"You'll understand one day," she said. That's the only explanation I ever got.

There was a flurry of ridiculous stuff on the news and then everyone ignored "whatever had happened." But not me. It changed my life. Mom left for a super secret meeting that she could not tell me about. I was left with Dad's telescope, my sweet Aunt Mabel, and homework. I was eleven. *It was only a matter of time...*